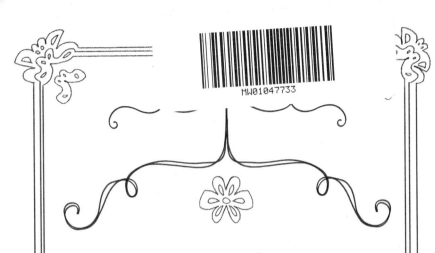

The Complete
Brontë Sisters
Children's Collection

Charlotte, Emily and Anne Brontë

Published by Sweet Cherry Publishing Limited
Unit 36, Vulcan House,
Vulcan Road,
Leicester, LE5 3EF
United Kingdom

First published in the UK in 2022
2022 edition

2 4 6 8 10 9 7 5 3 1

ISBN: 978-1-78226-711-9

The Complete Brontë Sisters Children's Collection:
Villette

Based on the original story by Charlotte Brontë,
adapted by Stephanie Baudet.

Cover design by Arianna Bellucci and Amy Booth
Illustrations by Arianna Bellucci

Lexile® code numerical measure L = Lexile® 700L

www.sweetcherrypublishing.com

Printed and bound in Turkey
T.OP005

Villette

Charlotte Brontë

Sweet Cherry

Chapter One

I was staying with my godmother, Madame Bretton, when I first met Paulina Home. Paulina was six years old and I, Lucy Snowe, was fourteen. I had no parents and she only had her father, who travelled a lot. Polly, as people called her, became very fond of Madame Bretton's son, John, who was sixteen.

After two months Polly's father, Mr Home, sent for her to go and live with him on the Continent. I left Madame Bretton's house soon after, and went to live with some distant relatives. The next eight years were not easy. One by one, my relatives all died. Having no one left to depend upon, I knew I must get work to support myself.

A lady called Miss Marchmont lived nearby. She was very rich, but couldn't walk because of her arthritis. She lived in two rooms at the top of her house.

One day she sent for me.

'My companion is getting married and will no longer be able to care for me,' she said, after we had drunk some tea. 'She will have her husband and house to look after. I heard that you have no family and I would like to offer you the job. It will not be easy. I need a lot of looking after.'

It did not take me long to decide. I felt comfortable with Miss Marchmont. She was never grumpy despite her pain, and I knew that she was a good woman.

And so, two stuffy rooms became my whole world.

Not many months after I started work, Miss Marchmont died in her sleep.

I was saddened by her death – another death to add to all the others I had suffered in my life. I had just fifteen pounds in my pocket, and decided to travel to

London. With no friends and no job, I felt alone and afraid. On the first night in London I cried myself to sleep.

I stayed at an inn near St Paul's Cathedral, where my father had stayed many years before. One day, I met an old schoolfriend, who had a French governess. She mentioned that in other countries, it was common to have an English governess. I thought I would easily find a job abroad, so I decided to travel to the Continent to look for work.

S.S.Vivid

1 adult. 2nd class.

London to Boue-Marine.

Departure: 8am.

On a black night, the coachman took me to the London docks. We had a rough crossing over the Channel. On the boat, I met Ginevra Fanshawe. Ginevra was seventeen and on her way to a girls' school in Villette. When we talked, she mentioned that there may be a job for me there.

I decided to go to Villette. I had nowhere else to go.

Chapter Two

It was night-time when I arrived at the school. I recognised the name of the owner on the door. Ginevra had told me about Madame Beck.

I rang the bell.

'May I see Madame Beck?' I asked the maid who opened the door.

She showed me up to a room. It felt cold, with the porcelain stove unlit and the bare polished floor. Golden ornaments stood on the mantelpiece either side of a clock, which chimed nine o'clock as I entered.

'You are English?' said a voice behind me, making me jump.

A motherly little woman in a large shawl and neat nightcap stood looking at me.

Madame Beck spoke hardly any English and I spoke no French, but

I made her understand that I was looking for work.

Then a small, thin man with glasses arrived. He was introduced as Monsieur Paul, Madame Beck's cousin and a teacher at the school. They both stared at me for a long time.

When Monsieur Paul left, Madame Beck had a meal brought to me, and I knew that I was welcome to stay. After eating, I was taken upstairs to a small room where three children were asleep in three tiny beds.

At a table a nursemaid sat fast asleep. Madame Beck didn't look pleased. She pointed me to a bed in one corner of the room, and left.

In the morning, the nursemaid who had been asleep at the table the night before was dismissed from her job. Madame Beck was very calm during the dismissal, and never once raised her voice.

The school had about one hundred day pupils and twenty boarders. There were twelve teachers, six servants and Madame Beck's three children. Madame Beck ran the school without any arguments. She crept around silently, watching people. If she found something wrong with the teachers or servants, they were quietly dismissed and new ones arrived.

She had sensible opinions and knew what was best for her pupils. They were well dressed and well fed. They had plenty of free time

and the lessons were not too strict. Behind the house was a large garden in which the girls had their lessons in the summer.

It was my job to look after and teach Madame Beck's children. However, one day, when a teacher was ill, Madame Beck asked me to teach an English class.

'I have never taught before, madame,' I said, nervously. The class had sixty pupils, and I knew they would laugh at my bad French.

Since arriving in Villette I had studied the language every evening, but I was far from fluent.

Madame Beck would not take no for an answer.

'Do you want to remain a nursemaid all your life?'

'No,' I said.

Madame Beck nodded. 'Remember that if you show any weakness, they will rule you.'

I walked into the classroom and faced the class. All of their eyes

were on me. They began to giggle and whisper.

I had never been so nervous in my life.

I began by asking one girl to read something she had written in English out loud. It was nonsense. Remembering Madame Beck's advice about not showing any weakness, I took the paper from her and calmly tore it in two.

It was against my nature, but I was determined to make a firm impression upon the girls. The class went quiet.

Madame Beck, who had been spying outside the door, was pleased. From that moment on, I was a teacher.

Chapter Three

The girl I had met on the ship, Ginevra Fanshawe, was a pupil at the school. We began to spend quite a lot of time together.

Whenever Ginevra was invited to a party, she would always wear a brand new dress. Then she would twirl in front of me and ask if she looked nice.

One day, as she showed off a particularly lovely dress, she told me that it had been bought by a lover. She had spoken of this man before, but I had not met him.

'It is wrong,' I said, 'to accept his presents if you do not plan to marry him.'

Ginevra just laughed and tossed her head.

Madame Beck was a strange person. She cared for her children very much, yet I never saw her hug or kiss them.

One day, little Fifine fell and broke her arm. The usual doctor was away so another one came instead. Doctor John was young,

and I thought he must be English because he spoke it so well. There was something familiar about him. I stared as I realised that he was Madame Bretton's son. I hadn't seen him for many years.

Everyone liked Doctor John. Though he became a frequent visitor, I never worked up the courage to speak to him.

In the summer the pupils put on a play for their families. After that came two months of hard study

before the pupils sat their exams.
Then came the long eight-week
holiday. Most of the pupils and
teachers went home or travelled.

I went on many long walks
around the city. At first, I was afraid
to go beyond the rue Fossette, but
gradually I went a little further and

explored beyond the city gates. I walked along little lanes, through fields and farms and woods. I often walked all day through the hot noon, the dry afternoon, and arrived home with moonrise.

As the time passed, I became very lonely. I thought of lively, happy Ginevra. She had recently admitted to me that Doctor John was the man who had bought her the beautiful dress. It was clear that Doctor John loved her, but she only enjoyed being admired. She had no interest in marrying him, and had been seen with a count she had met – Count de Hamal.

For many days I stayed in bed, feeling very ill. The stormy weather made me even feel worse and I often had nightmares. I did not know what was real and what wasn't.

One evening I got up and dressed, weak and shaky. I could not bear the loneliness and stillness of the long dormitory with its ghastly white beds anymore. The roof of the house seemed to press down on me. I had to get outside.

It was raining and windy. The church bells seemed to call out to me, so I went in. I knelt down with everyone else. It was a plain old church, the only colour coming from the light cast through the purple stained-glass windows.

When the service was over most of the people left. I went to the priest, and asked him for some advice and comfort. I talked with him about living on my own and being ill, and the way he kindly listened lifted my heart a little.

On my walk home, I became lost in an old part of the city. I wandered around for a long time, trying to find my way, trying to find my way. I started feeling ill as I wandered and then I fainted on the steps of a building.

Chapter Four

When I awoke and looked around,
it was as if I had gone back in
time to my childhood at my
godmother's house in England. I
saw familiar things all around me.
There were two blue china vases
on the mantlepiece. There was

an ornament of two white horses,

covered in glass. There were some

pictures I had drawn!

'Where am I?' I murmured.

A woman stood up and walked

towards me from the other side

of the room. She didn't speak, but bathed my forehead with cool, perfumed water and made me comfortable. She gave me some medicine, then sat back down and carried on knitting.

When I awoke again I was in a different room – one I did not recognise except for the painting of a boy hanging on the wall. I had seen the painting many times.

'John,' I whispered.

'Do you want my son?' asked a voice.

It was Madame Bretton herself.

'He recognised you when he found you collapsed on the steps of the church, and carried you here. He told me you are an English teacher at a school here. You have been unwell for many days, my dear.'

I realised that she didn't recognise me, and I was puzzled as to what she was doing here in Villette. But I was too tired to think about it, and quickly fell asleep again.

It was evening when I awoke, and I felt much stronger. I got up and dressed myself. Madame Bretton was surprised but pleased, and helped me downstairs.

I watched her carefully, and realised that she must now be fifty. She still seemed just as I remembered her.

Then, Doctor John arrived. 'Are you feeling better?' he asked me.

'Much better, thank you, Doctor John.'

He had not changed a lot either. But, like his mother, it seemed that he didn't remember me.

As the evening went on, Madame Bretton kept glancing at me. At last she said, 'John, does this young lady remind you of someone?'

He looked at me and shook his head.

I worked up my courage, and said 'I am Lucy Snowe.'

41

'I knew it!' cried Madame Bretton.

She stepped forwards to kiss me.

'How could I not see it?' exclaimed Doctor John. He looked astonished. 'Mamma calls me a stupid boy,' he said. 'And I think I am. I have seen you plenty of times at the school but never recognised you. I see it now!'

I smiled. 'Do you remember when you first came to the school and I stared at you until you became cross?'

'Now I know why!' he said, laughing.

Chapter Five

Madame Bretton, Doctor John and myself chatted all evening long. We caught up on everything that had been happening in our lives in the years since we had last met.

John had done well in his career, and had bought a big house in the countryside not far from Villette. His mother had moved here soon after.

John said I had been very ill, and he ordered me to have more rest. He kindly led me to the door and held up the candle to light my way up the stairs.

My godmother looked after me well. She brought meals up to me herself. The room was always cheerier with her in it. I was so much happier now that I had friends with me.

John talked about Ginevra as if she were an angel with no faults. I tried to tell him otherwise, but he did not want to hear.

'She is touring with her friends in the south of France,' I said.

'Do you know when she will be back?'

'She doesn't tell me all of her plans,' I said, almost losing my patience.

Madame Beck came to visit me during this time. John told her that

I was not ready for work yet, and I stayed at the Bretton's house for two weeks longer than the holidays.

One evening, the three of us went to a concert at which the King, Queen and Prince were present. My godmother had a beautiful pink dress made for me, but I was embarrassed to wear such a bold colour. I wished I could wear brown velvet like my godmother instead. John gave me a

small bouquet of flowers and smiled
at my dress, which made me feel a
bit better.

SATURDAY 12TH OCTOBER AT 8PM.

Villette Conservatoire for Young
Ladies proudly presents a variety
concert performed by the students.

It will be followed by a lottery to
raise funds for the poor of the city.

The concert will be graced by the presence
of their majesties, the King and Queen,
and their son, the Prince.

The concert was held in a grand hall with a high arched golden ceiling. Crystal chandeliers hung down, sparkling like shivering rainbows.

It was full of ladies wearing fine dresses, and gentlemen in their evening clothes.

I saw Monsieur Paul helping his brother, Josef, who was one of the best music teachers in Villette. Monsieur Paul was enjoying standing on the stage in front of all these grand people. I smiled to myself as I watched him organise the girls.

At last, all was ready. Only one box, with regal chairs and red curtains, remained empty.

Then everyone stood up as the royal party entered.

I had never seen a king or queen before, and was a little disappointed when an old grey-haired man entered with a younger woman at his side. The king looked pale and a little nervous. His wife was graceful and elegant, but she also looked displeased.

I then recognised two of Madame Beck's pupils in the royal box too. And there was Ginevra!

I glanced at John and knew that he had seen her too.

Ginevra looked over at us and stared at Madame Bretton through small binoculars. She made a sneering remark to the lady next to her, and they both started to laugh.

When the concert was over, John turned to me. 'You were right about Ginevra,' he said. 'It was so cruel of her to make fun of my mother.'

'Oh, I'm sure she doesn't mean it,' I said. 'She's just a silly school girl.'

He shook his head angrily. 'I saw the way she and Count de Hamal looked at each other when they met in the foyer. It was a sort of secret understanding.'

On our way out we met Monsieur Paul. He looked at my dress curiously. I tried to ignore him looking at me, but I could not.

Chapter Six

At last, it was time for me to go back to the school. I was very sad to leave my godmother and John. I would miss both of them terribly. John said he would write to me, but I was sure he would be too busy. When I got to my room that evening I cried myself to sleep.

The next morning I was still upset, and Monsieur Paul saw the tears on my cheeks. He was very sympathetic and I saw just what a kind man he was. He didn't say anything to

embarrass me, but the softening of his expression gave me comfort.

I went to my classroom five minutes before the pupils arrived. Then, Ginevra Fanshawe rushed in.

'Was Doctor John angry at me?' she asked mischievously. 'What did he say about me making fun of his mother?'

She was a selfish girl who could not imagine other peoples' feelings, but I knew that she did not mean to be cruel.

'What is fun to you can hurt others,' I said, sternly.

She giggled and danced around excitedly.

John did send me a letter, as promised. I saved it the whole day so I could read and enjoy it on my own. I took a candle and went up to the attic. It was cold up there, but private. I wrapped myself in my shawl.

I broke the seal and took out
the letter. I read it slowly. John
reminded me of all the places we
had gone and the things we had
talked about when I was staying
with him and his mother.

It was a simple letter, yet it gave
me the greatest joy.

Suddenly, I heard footsteps.

I held up my candle and saw
a shadowy figure standing in the
middle of the room. It wore a
straight black robe and a white veil.

I screamed. I ran down the stairs, bursting into Madame Beck's sitting room. She had several guests, including Doctor John.

'There is something in the attic!'

I realised that I had left the letter upstairs. I had to get it. I ran back with Madame Beck, her guests following.

I felt cold and shaky as we entered the room again. The letter was not there.

Then a voice behind me spoke my name. It was John. 'Was it my letter?' he asked.

'Yes,' I said. 'I cannot bear to lose it!'

He took my cold hand in his warm one and led me downstairs. Then he took my letter from his waistcoat pocket. He had found it on the floor and had been teasing me.

'What did you see?' he asked. I was afraid of being laughed at, but I told him about the figure I had seen. John looked at me with surprise, and told me that many years ago, the school had been a convent. There was a story that a nun had been buried alive in the garden. Some people believed that they had seen her ghost.

Chapter Seven

During the next three weeks John sent me four more letters, which I kept together in a little box. We

visited my godmother together once a week.

One evening we went to the theatre. At the most exciting part of the play, there came the sudden sound of rushing feet and frantic voices backstage.

A flame. A smell of smoke.

'Fire!'

Then came panic. People began to rush from the theatre.

A young women near us got caught in the stampede, and separated from her father. John pushed back through the crowd to reach her, and managed to get her outside to safety.

John, Madame Bretton and I went back to the young woman's apartment with her and her father. There, John checked that she wasn't hurt.

After that came seven weeks when I did not hear from John at all. Every day I waited for a letter, but none came.

Then, one day, I walked into my classroom to find a letter on my desk. It was not from John, but from his mother.

Dear Lucy,

I expect that you have been busy this last two months, just as we have. John has gained many new patients.

I know that Thursday is your half-day off. Please be ready at five o'clock and I will send the carriage to bring you here, where you will meet an old friend.

Very truly yours,

Louisa Bretton

I instantly cheered up. I could not wait for my day with them.

On Thursday afternoon it began to snow heavily. As I watched for the carriage, I feared it would not come.

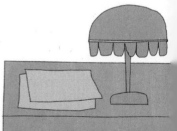

The white storm raged so thickly that it was difficult to see the road.

Finally, the carriage arrived. Once I reached my godmother's house I ran straight up to the sitting room. There was a blazing fire in the hearth. Madame Bretton hugged me tightly.

Then, I heard someone enter the room. To my surprise, I turned to see the young woman from the theatre.

She smiled slowly. 'You do not know me, do you?'

'We met some weeks ago, when the theatre caught fire. I hope you are feeling better,' I said. But as I looked at her fine, delicate face, a memory stirred.

'You have forgotten,' she said in a soft voice. 'I once sat on your knee and even shared your pillow. Do you remember Mr Home?'

I nodded. 'You are little Polly.'

'Yes, but my name has changed. My father inherited an estate and a title. My name is now Paulina Home de Bassompierre.'

Polly had become beautiful a young woman of seventeen.

Madame Bretton looked on fondly. 'Polly and her father visited us after the fire at the theatre. It was only when she recognised my mirror and my pincushion, that we realised who she and her father were,' she said.

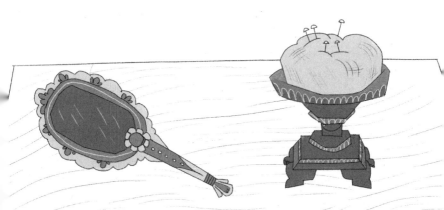

Doctor John arrived later in the evening, with Polly's father. The two men looked like mountains of snow on their horses.

'Father! You look like an enormous polar bear!' Polly laughed as she helped him off with his coat in the kitchen.

We all had a wonderful evening together, despite the winter night howling outside. It was just like years ago in England, when John, Polly and I had been friends as children. We had so much to catch up on.

One day the letters I had received from Doctor John disappeared from my drawer. I knew that Madame Beck had 'borrowed' them to read. When they were returned the next day I sealed them in a jar. Once it was dark, I went out and buried the jar in the root of an old tree. I knew it was Madame Beck's habit to know everything that was going on with her staff and pupils, but I did not want her reading my private letters.

As I turned to go back inside, I saw a figure nearby. A nun, dressed in a black robe and white veil. I could feel her looking at me.

Summoning my courage, I spoke to her.

She continued to stand in silence, before finally fading into the bushes, almost like a ghost.

Chapter Eight

The first of March was Monsieur Paul's birthday. Everyone in the school gave him little bunches of flowers. The pile on his desk was so high that he was hidden behind it.

Because I did not like picked flowers, I did not give him any. It was such a shame to cut short their beauty and cause their slow wilting and death.

Later that evening Mr Paul said to me, 'When it is your birthday, I will give you a present.'

I smiled. 'As I give you one.' I took a small box out of my pocket and handed it to him.

He noticed his initials scratched on the top. Carefully, he opened the box and took out the little chain I had made, all glossy with silk and sparkling with beads.

'You made this for me?' he asked.

I could see that he liked it.

He pulled his pocket watch out of his pocket, tying one end of the chain to it, and the other to his waistcoat.

It wasn't long before spring came, and the weather suddenly got warmer.

One Sunday afternoon, having walked all the way back from church, I went into my deserted classroom. Warm and tired from

the walk, I rested my head in my
folded arms on my desk and fell
asleep. Two hours later I awoke.
Someone had put a soft shawl
under my head and another around
my shoulders.

It was the kind of thing Madame Beck would do.

I decided to have a walk in the garden before dark. In the alley, I listened to the hum of bees and admired the blossom.

I leant against the trunk of the great old tree where I had buried the letters from John. He was a kind, affectionate man, but I realised now that while we cared for each other deeply, it was not a romantic love. We were family.

'Goodnight, Mademoiselle,' said a voice.

I jumped. Turning around, I saw Monsieur Paul.

'I hope you slept well?' he asked. 'That desk must have been hard.'

'It was you,' I smiled, as he walked with me along the alley. 'Thank you for the shawls.'

After a few moments of silence he said, 'I have seen strange things in this garden.' He leant against a tree and puffed at his cigar as he watched me. 'Do you know the legend of this house?'

I nodded. 'They say that hundreds of years ago a nun was buried alive in this garden. Her ghost haunts the grounds.'

'I have seen her,' he said.

'So have I, Monsieur.'

The prayer bell rang in the house. Suddenly, a figure ran out, sweeping past us. It was the nun herself.

The wind rose to a howl. Rain started pouring down, wild and

cold. Monsieur Paul grabbed
my hand, and we rushed inside
together.

Chapter Nine

Polly and her father, Count de Bassompierre, had just arrived back from travelling around Europe. She invited me to her house and told me all about their travels.

She also talked a lot about John. She had received a letter

from him while away. In it, he confessed his love for her. It was clear that Polly loved him too. Her face was alive and her eyes sparkled. But her father did not yet know and she worried that he might not approve. Having only his doctor's wage, there would be richer men who were interested in Polly.

One warm day in early May, all of the teachers and boarders went out to breakfast in the countryside.

We wore summer dresses instead
of our dull school dresses. Monsieur

Paul looked cheerful in a light shirt and straw hat.

The streets were quiet and the fields peaceful as we walked by. Ginevra walked with me and leant heavily on my arm. Monsieur Paul kept smiling at me, teasing me about my pretty dress.

At last we reached a small hill surrounded by trees. We all sat on the green grass as Monsieur Paul told us a story. He was very good at story-telling and everyone was enthralled.

Once he had finished, we went to a nearby farmhouse where coffee was made, rolls buttered and plenty of eggs supplied.

Monsieur Paul smiled and watched as everyone ate and talked. He was always happy when making others happy.

After the meal, the younger children went to play while the teachers helped tidy up.

Monsieur Paul asked me to come and sit with him under a tree. I read to him.

Then he asked if I would miss him if he went away for a year or two.

The thought brought tears to my eyes. He told me he had sudden urgent matters to take care of, and would be leaving Europe soon.

I hid my face with the book so he would not see my tears.

The following week I went into the town on my free afternoon to try to forget my misery. Madame Beck had given me a list of things to buy for the pupils and a basket of flowers to deliver to a friend whose birthday it was.

This friend was a rude old woman. The maid tried to stop me entering the house, but a kind priest, who was also visiting, persuaded her to let me in.

After delivering the flowers to the ungrateful woman, a violent storm stopped me from leaving the house. I sat in a small room with the priest. Soon I realised that he was the same kind priest to whom I had poured my heart out the previous year, when I had been alone and depressed.

While the storm raged outside, he told me the story of the young man who had wanted to marry the old woman's granddaughter, Marie. The old woman had not allowed it, and the girl had gone into a convent and died soon after. The poor man still gave more than half his salary to the grandmother each month, even though she was the cause of his unhappiness. Twenty years later, he still came to the house to gaze at the picture of the young woman on the mantlepiece.

'Monsieur Paul is the man, isn't he?' I guessed.

The priest nodded. 'He is a good man, Miss Snowe. I would not like anyone to take advantage of his kindness.'

When I next saw Monsieur Paul, I told him that I knew the story of his great love, Marie. He took my hand and asked if we could still be friends. I felt my heart break, but I nodded. I understood that he hadn't got over his first love.

Chapter Ten

John eventually asked Polly's father for his permission to marry her. While he was sad to lose his little girl, Polly's father knew that John truly loved her, and he trusted him.

The week following the engagement, Madame Beck announced that

Monsieur Paul would not be teaching at the school anymore. He was going away on a long trip to Guadeloupe, in the West Indies. The halls were quickly alive with gossip from the girls about why he was leaving.

A few days before the announcement, Monsieur Paul and I had gone on a walk together. We spoke for a long time, and he asked me what I wanted to do with my life. I told him that I had been thinking about opening my own school.

He took my hand and
pulled me towards him.
He looked at me with what
I knew must be love.

Suddenly, two people
appeared around the
corner. It was
Madame
Beck and
the priest.

The priest
was angry.

He disapproved of Monsieur Paul's friendship with me, and I suddenly realised that this must be why Monsieur Paul was leaving.

On the last day, Monsieur Paul said goodbye to everyone at the school. When he searched for me, Madame Beck pulled him away.

I could not bear it. What should I do without him? I loved him more than I had realised.

The bell went and everyone left, leaving me standing alone in my misery.

After a few minutes, a small
child came in and handed me a
note.

'Monsieur Paul said I was to find
you and give this to you,' she said.

I thanked the girl, and opened
the letter as soon as she had gone.

I missed you today. I must see you
before I sail.
Paul

The next morning I could not hide my face, red and swollen from crying.

Weeks later, after I was sure his ship must have sailed, Monsieur Paul came to me. Dressed in his travelling clothes, he rushed towards me, took my hand and looked into my eyes.

'Paul!' shouted a voice behind us. It was Madame Beck. Her eyes were like steel as she looked at me.

'Leave us!' said Monsieur Paul.

'I will send for the priest!' she said. 'This is not right.'

Then she saw the angry look on Monsieur Paul's face. She left.

'You must know that I wouldn't go without saying goodbye,' he said. 'I would not forget you for a single minute.'

We walked outside together. Monseiur Paul said he planned to stay away for three years to help the widow of an old friend to manage her estate and get it running well. He asked me if I still wanted to open a little school while he was away.

We reached a street outside the town centre and stopped by a small, pretty house. Monsieur Paul took a key from his pocket and opened the door. The house was freshly painted and furnished.

'What a lovely place,' I said. We walked into a spacious, bare room. Monsieur Paul took a sheet of paper from his pocket and put it into my hand.

School for Young Ladies,
Number 7, Fauberg Clotilde.
Director: Mademoiselle Lucy Snowe.

At first, I was speechless. This was my dream. Then, I couldn't stop asking questions.

Monsieur Paul had rented the house and furnished it. He had printed some advertisements for the new school too, and put them around the town.

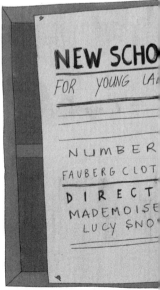

'This is what I have been doing these last three weeks,' he said. 'You can keep busy here until I come back.' He stroked my hair. 'One day you shall share my life.'

We walked back to the school hand in hand, and said goodbye.

Epilogue

Over the next few years, I worked hard in my little school and was very happy. Monsieur Paul sent me a letter with every ship he sailed on.

Polly and Doctor John lived a happy life together, just as she had hoped as a child. They had a son together and several daughters.

I found out, to my relief, that the 'ghost' I had seen in the attic and in the garden had been Count Hamel in disguise. He had been visiting Ginevra in secret. The two lovers eventually ran away to be married, and had a much-loved son.

Charlotte, Emily and Anne Bronte were three incredible women. Now, over two centuries since the sisters lived, their books are still amongst the most popular in the world.

Brought up in the lonely Yorkshire moors, Charlotte, Emily and Anne Bronte are poor and motherless. Charlotte is strong and longs to travel, Emily is shy and prefers the company of animals over people, and Anne is the gentlest of them all. Despite their differences, all three sisters have big imaginations and even bigger dreams. And all are determined for their voices to be heard.